First American edition 1986

First published by Thomas Nelson Australia.
First impression
Printed in Hong Kong by South China Printing Co.
Library of Congress Cataloging-in-Publication Data
Allen, Pamela.
A lion in the night.
Summary: A royal household is disrupted
when a lion runs off with the baby.
[1. Lions—Fiction. 2. Babies—Fiction] I. Title.
PZ7.A433Li 1986 [E] 85-12346
ISBN 0-399-21203-5

A Lion in the Night

Pamela Allen

G. P. Putnam's Sons New York

THERE ONCE WAS a baby who lived
in a castle with the King, the Queen,
the Admiral, the Captain, the General,
the Sergeant, and the little dog.

Because she was the baby
she couldn't walk, and she couldn't talk.
But she could cry.

One night, when she had been
put to bed while it was still light,
she made a wish.

Later, when the moon was out
and the tide was high,
the Queen woke up.
And what did she see?

She saw a lion stealing the baby.

The Queen
woke the King,
and

the King
woke the Admiral,

and
the Admiral
woke the Captain,

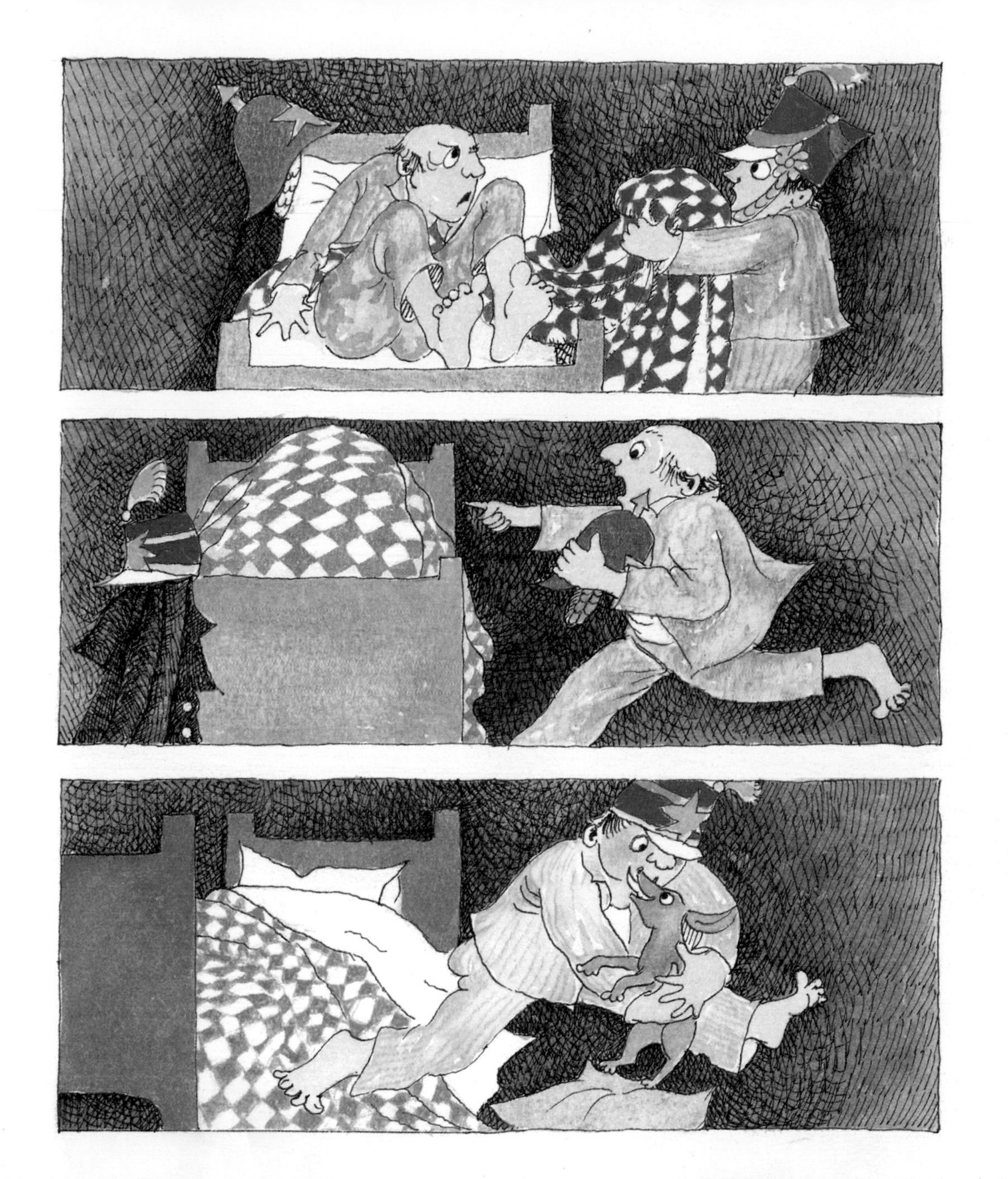

and
the Captain
woke the General,

and
the General
woke the Sergeant,

and
the Sergeant
woke the little dog,
and
WHAT DID THEY DO?

They *chased* the lion.
The lion that was stealing the baby.

yip
yip
yip

Out of the forest
and past the church.

Past the church
and into the boat.

Into the boat
and across the sea.

Across the sea
and over the mountains.

yip
yip
yip
yip
yip
yip
yip

Over the mountains
and into the fields.

And there the lion stopped.

yip
yip
yip

Grrrrrrrrrr......

RRRA
YOWL

AH

Back home
they ran
as fast as they could.
Over the mountains
into the boat
across the sea
past the church
into the forest
and through the fields

but . . .

GGRRRRR
clik
clik
clik
yip
yip
yip

"Ha! Ha! I'm the King of the castle
and you're the dirty rascals," bellowed the lion.

He'd got there first and fooled them all.

Now the game was over, everyone except the lion
and the baby was very tired. And everyone
as well as the lion and the baby was very hungry.
So the lion invited them all in for breakfast.

They had what they usually had for breakfast;
all except the lion, who gave the baby her bottle,
tied a napkin around his neck,
then gobbled up . . .
. . . one bowl of porridge,

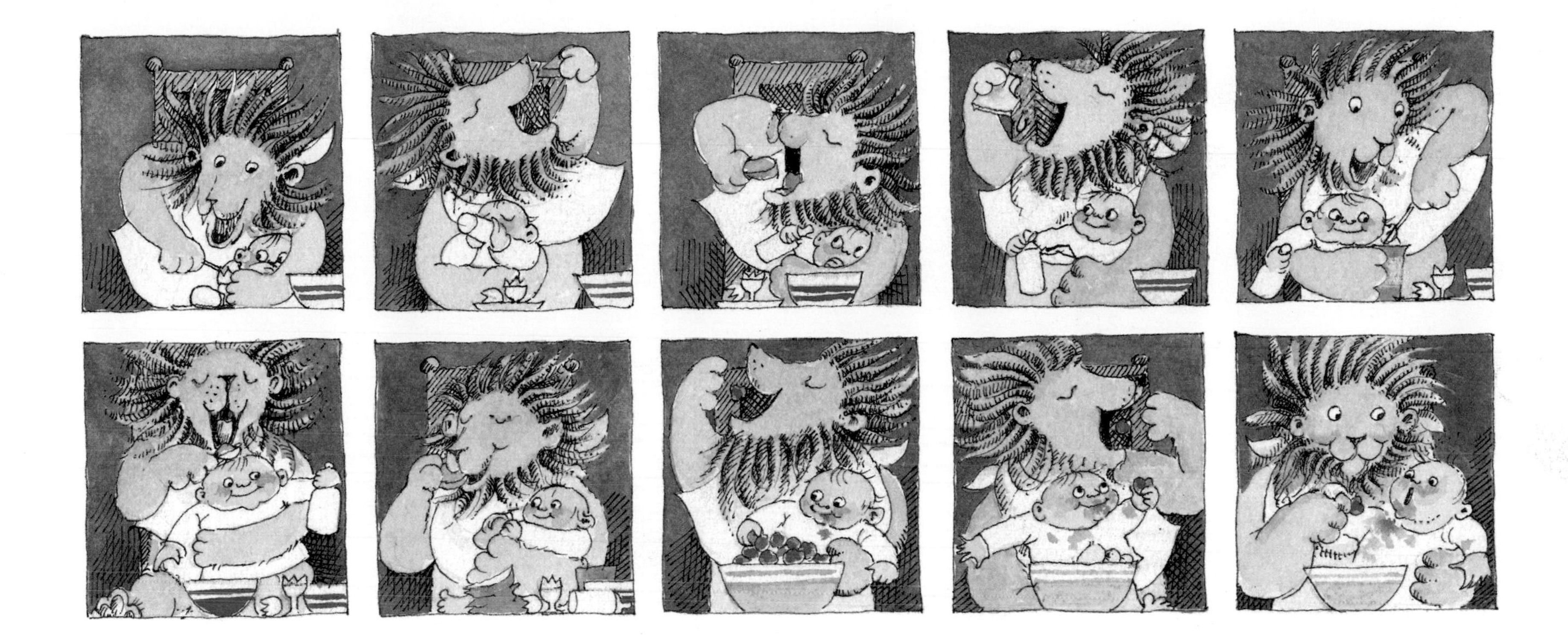

two eggs, a slice of hot buttered toast,
some crumpets, bread and honey, fruit yogurt,
muesli, a bag of biscuits belonging to the
little dog, and last of all,
a big bowl of strawberries and red Jell-O.

Then, because it was morning

the lion . . .

just disappeared.